A FOX JUMPED UP ONE WINTER'S NIGHT

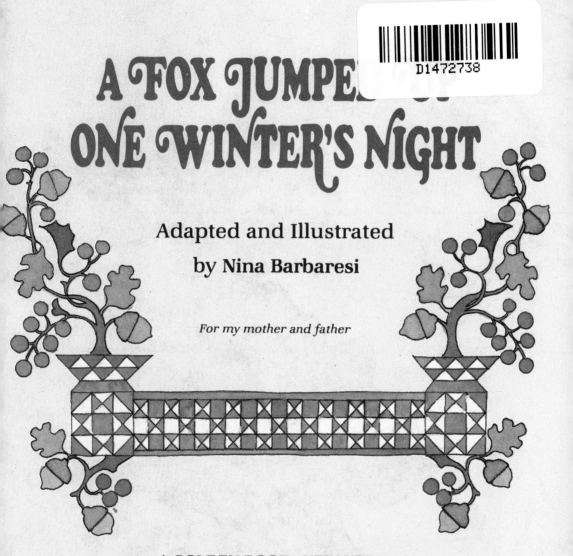

Adapted and Illustrated
by Nina Barbaresi

For my mother and father

A GOLDEN BOOK · NEW YORK
Western Publishing Company, Inc., Racine, Wisconsin 53404

A fox jumped up one winter's night
And begged the moon to give him light,
For he'd many miles to run that night
Before he'd reach his den, O!
Den, O! Den, O!

For he'd many miles to run that night

Before he'd reach his den, O!

He ran up to a pen of geese,
And thought, "Now *here*'s a tempting
  feast!
I'll leave one dollar bill at least
In payment for one bird, O!
Bird, O! Bird, O!
I'll leave one dollar bill at least
In payment for one bird, O!"

He caught a gray goose by the neck
And swung her right across his back.
The gray goose cried out, "Quack, quack, quack!"
With her legs all dangling down, O!
Down, O! Down, O!

The gray goose cried out, "Quack, quack, quack!"
With her legs all dangling down, O!

Old Mother Giggle-Gaggle jumped out of bed,
And out of the window she popped her head.
She cried, "John! John! A gray goose is gone,
And the fox is on the run, O!
Run, O! Run, O!"

She cried, "John! John! A gray goose is gone,
And the fox is on the run, O!"

John ran up to the top of the hill
And blew his horn both loud and shrill.
Said the fox, "That's pretty music, still,
I'd rather be in my den, O!
Den, O! Den, O!"

Said the fox, "That's pretty music, still,
I'd rather be in my den, O!"

The fox ran back to his cozy den
And his dear little foxes, eight, nine, ten.
They said, "Daddy, *please* go back again
To that wonderful, cheerful farm, O!
Farm, O! Farm, O!"
They said, "Daddy, *please* go back again
To that wonderful, cheerful farm, O!"

The fox and his wife, without any strife,
Served up the goose with a fork and knife.
They'd never eaten so well in their life,
And the little ones chewed on the bones, O!
Bones, O! Bones, O!

They'd never eaten so well in their life

And the little ones chewed on the bones, O!

A Fox Jumped Up
One Winter's Night